P9-CBS-606

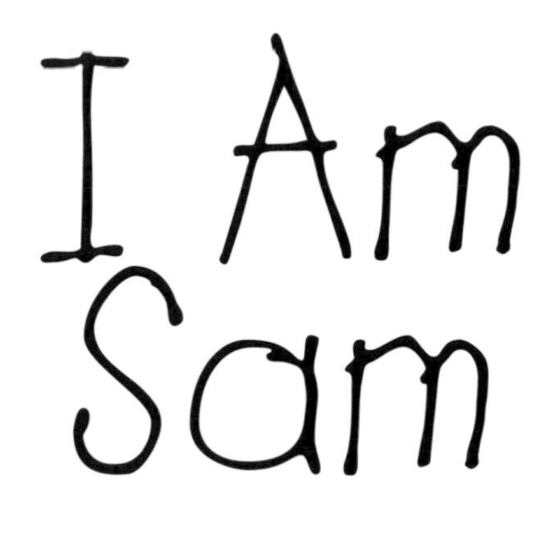

visit us at www.flyingrhino.com

Mailing Address: P.O. Box 3989
Portland, Oregon
97208-3989

E-mail Address: bigfan@flyingrhino.com

Library of Congress Control Number:
98-094851

ISBN 1-883772-15-X

Printed in Mexico

I am Sam.

I am Sam. Sam the Ram.
I like to count.

I see one dog.

I spy two frogs.

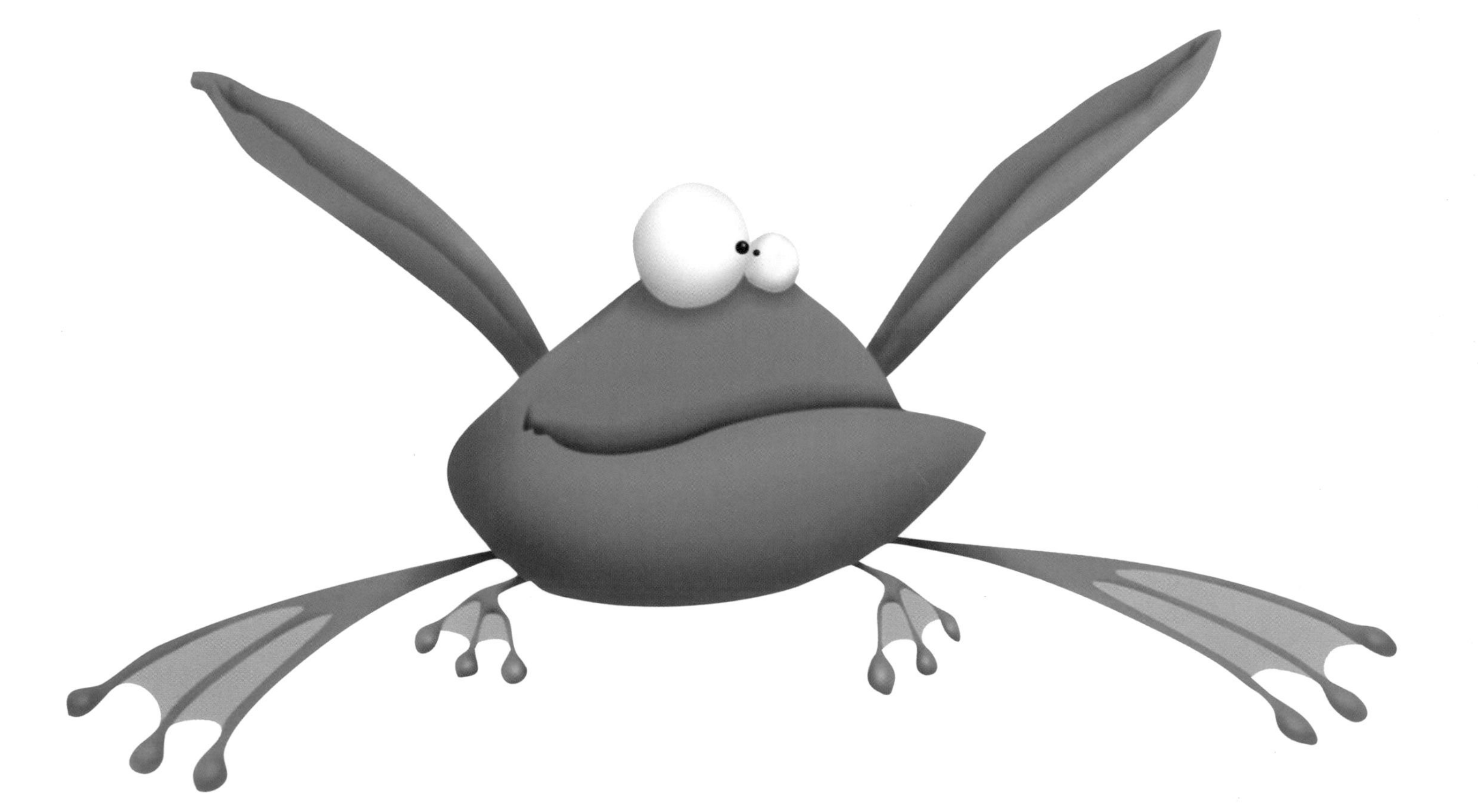

I see three cows.

I spot four sows.

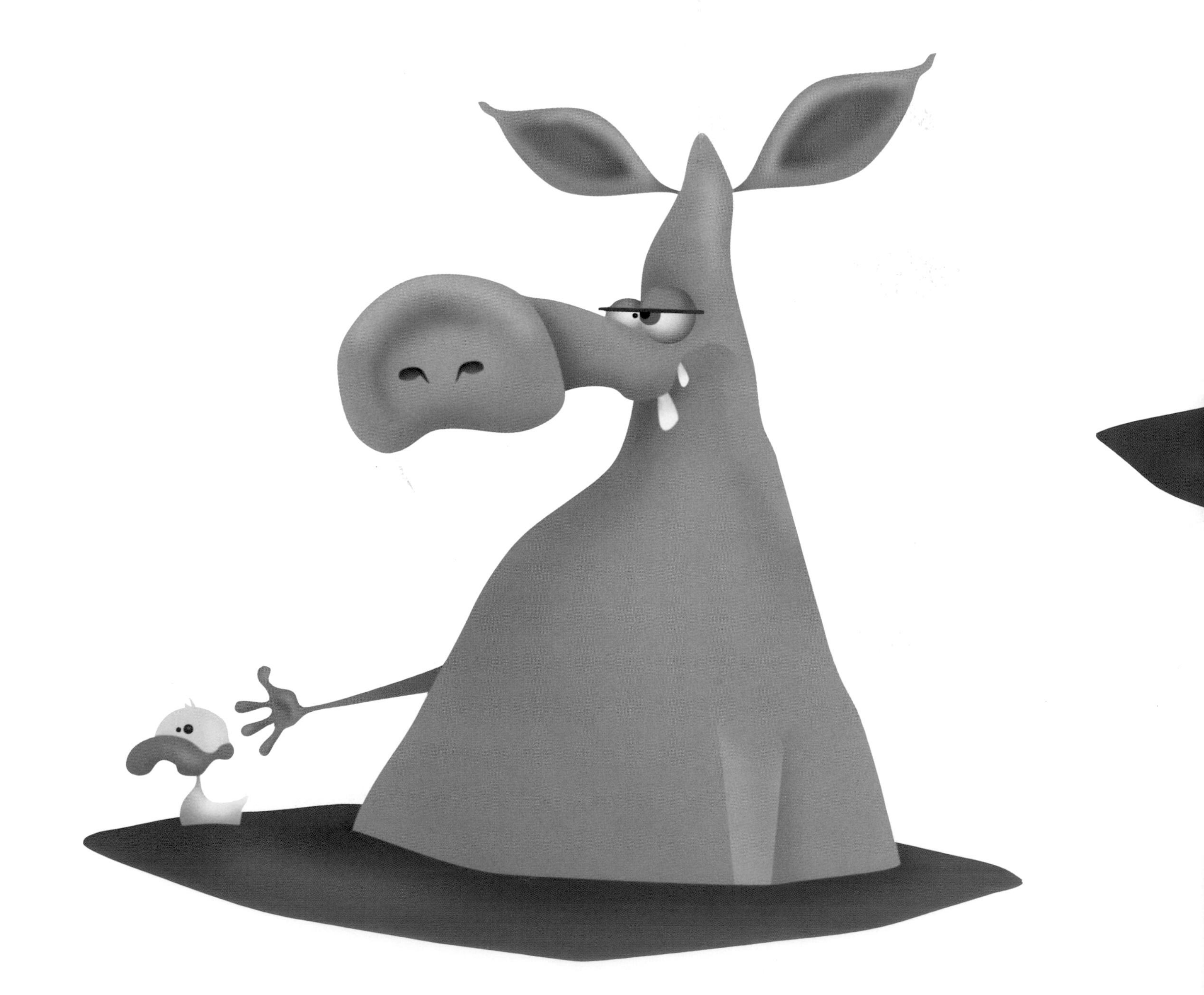

I see five sheep.

I hear six chicks say
peep, peep, peep.

Peep!

Peep!

Peep!

Peep!
Peep!

I see seven cats.

I see eight rats.

I see nine fish. Five are blue
and four are red.

I see ten ducks flying overhead.

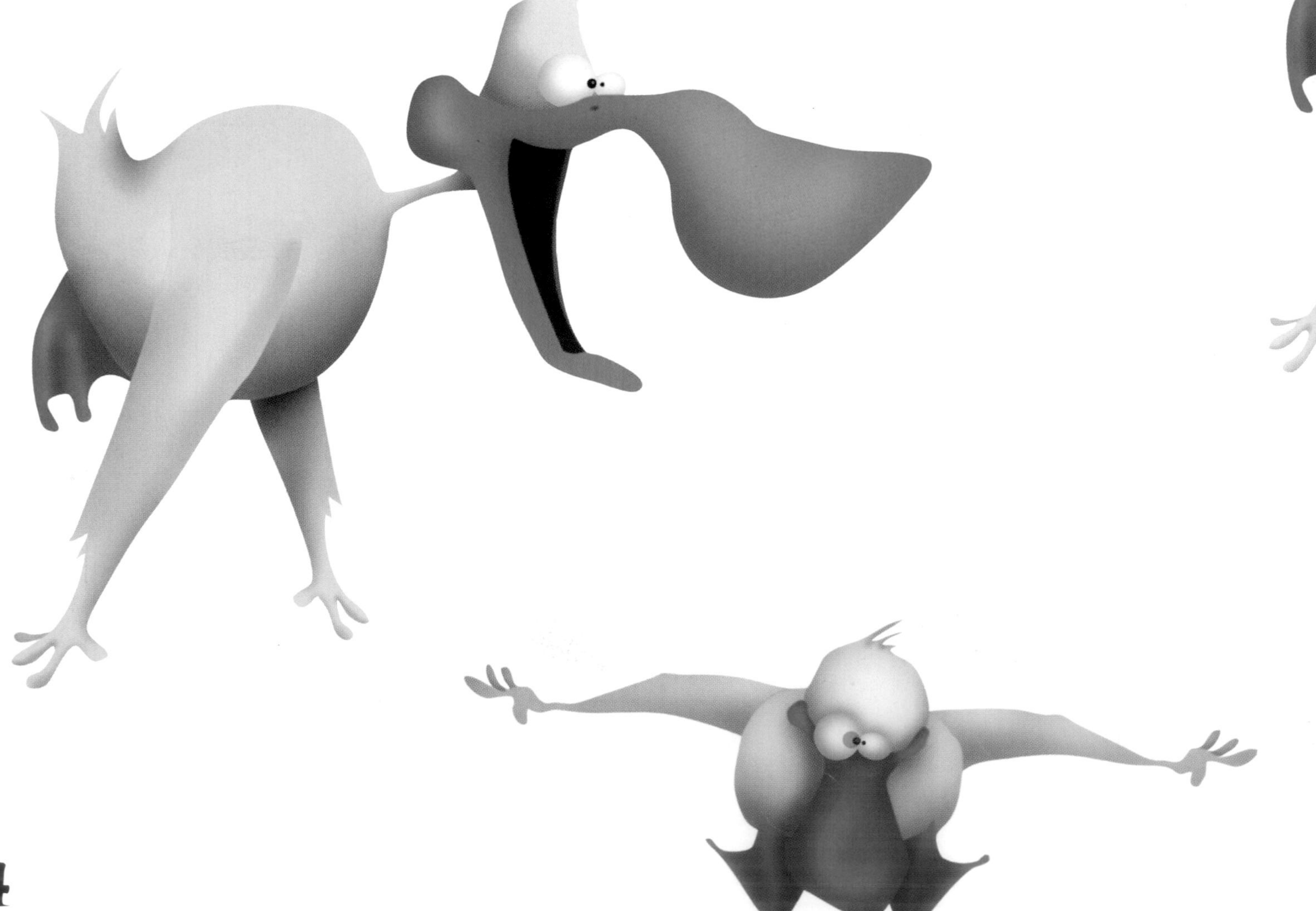

Oh me! Oh my!
A big, blue bull
has caught my eye.

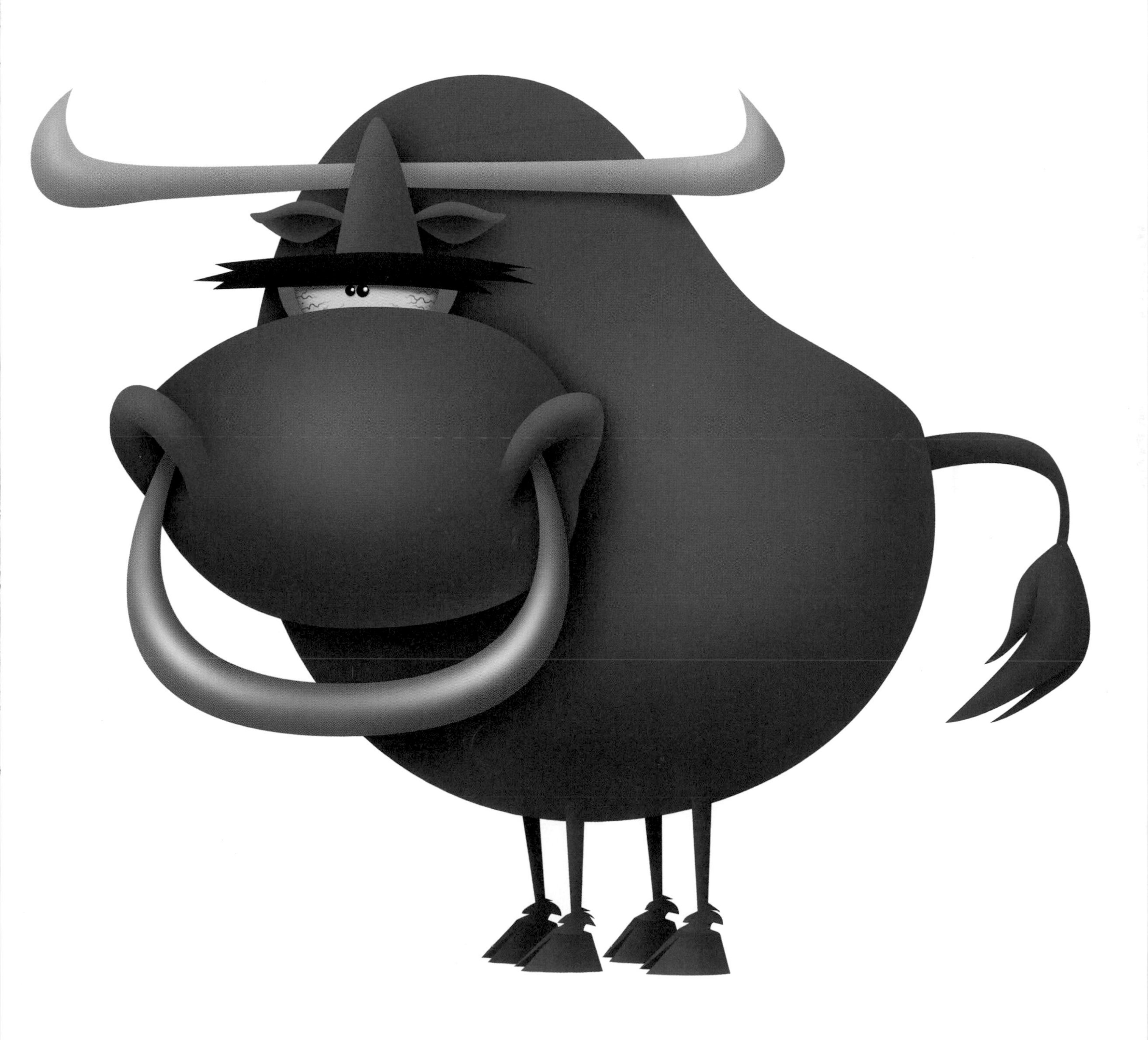

My counting time has been fun.
But now it's time for me to run!

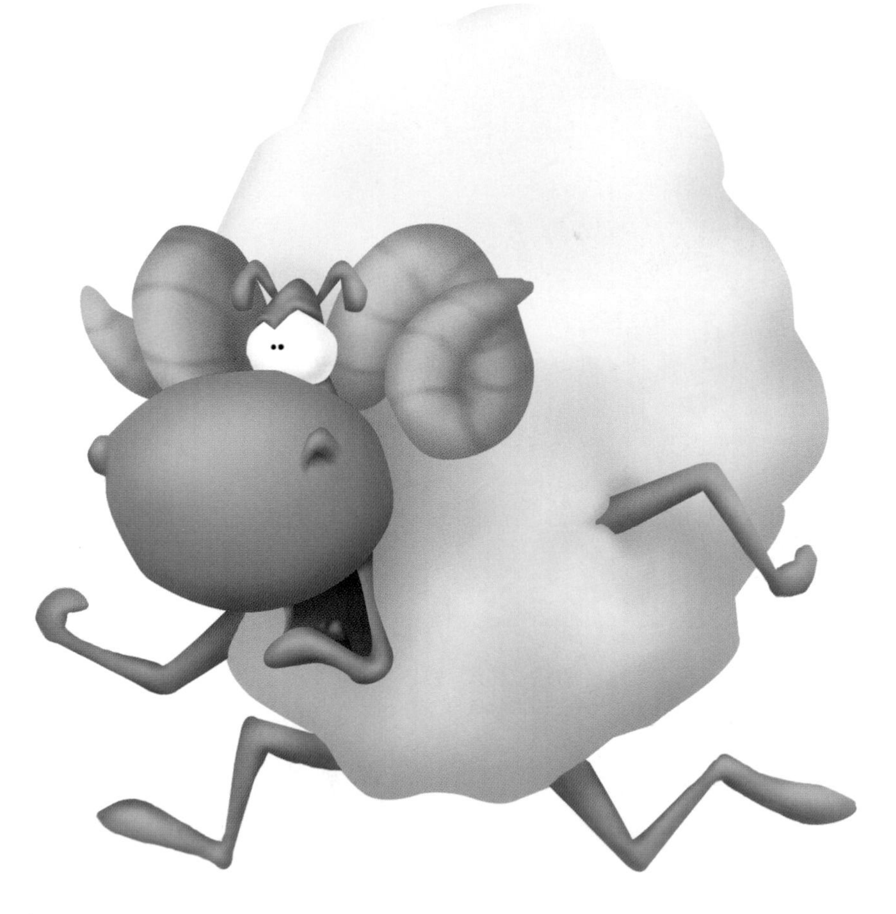

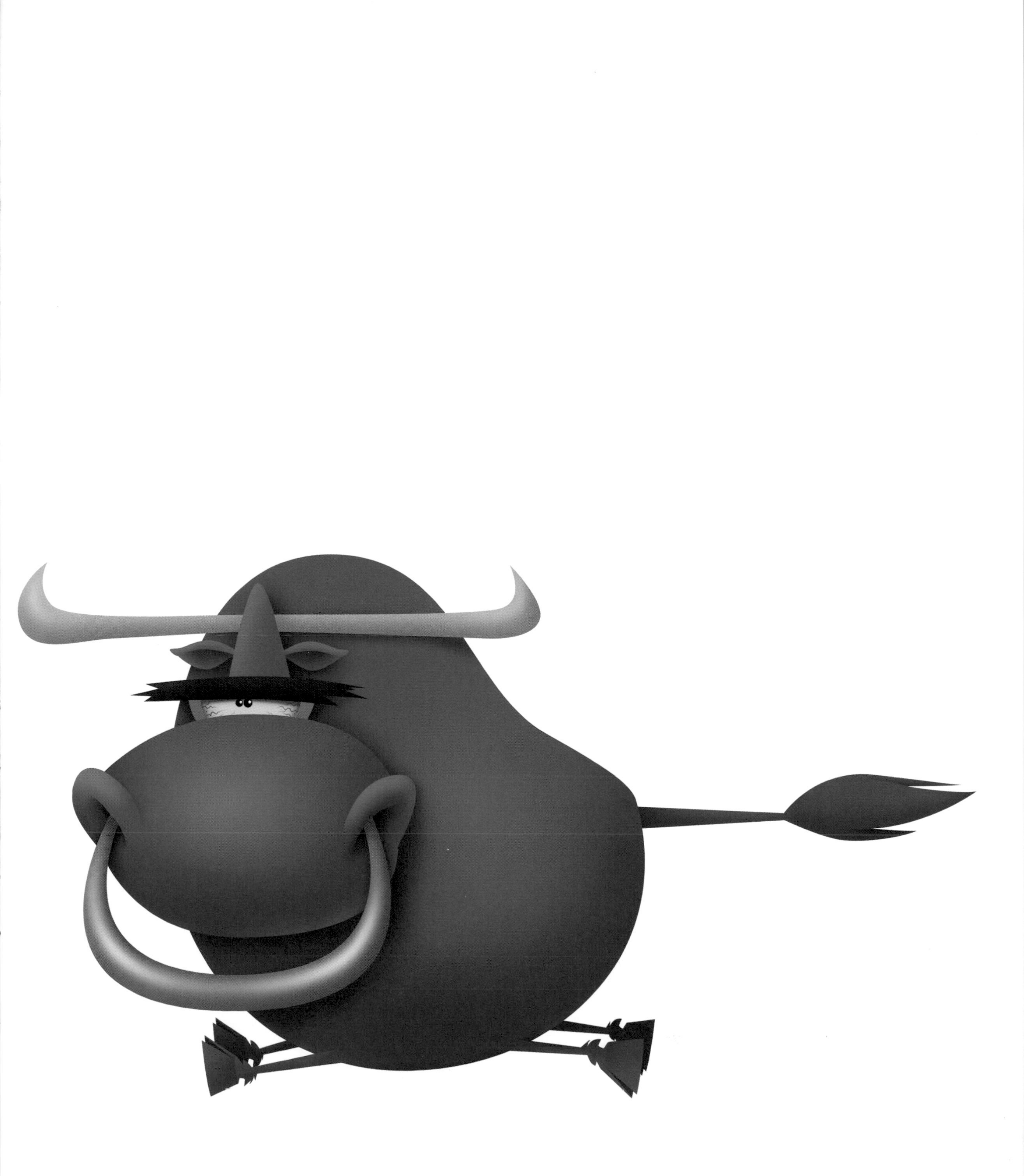

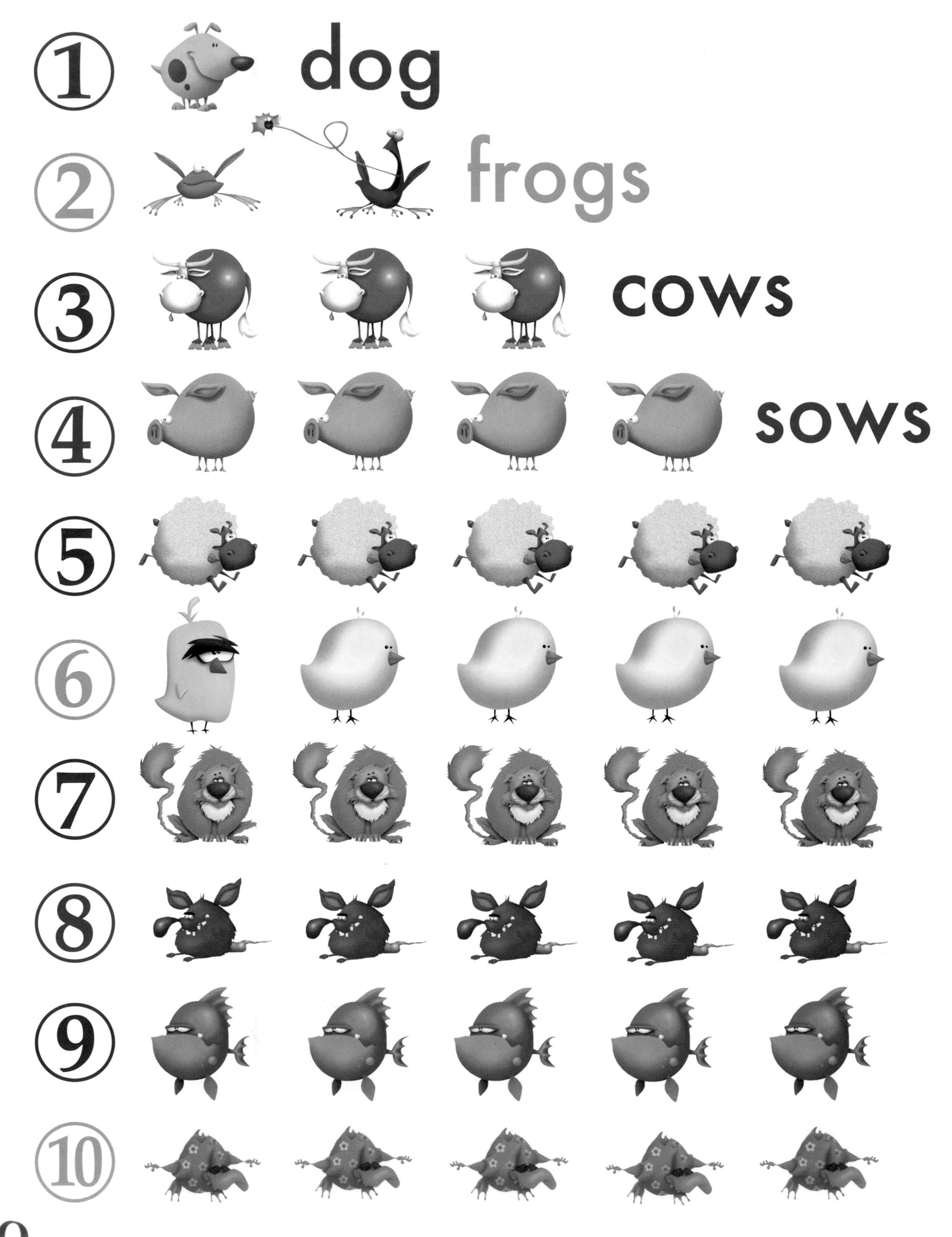
1 dog
2 frogs
3 cows
4 sows
5
6
7
8
9
10

GLOSSARY

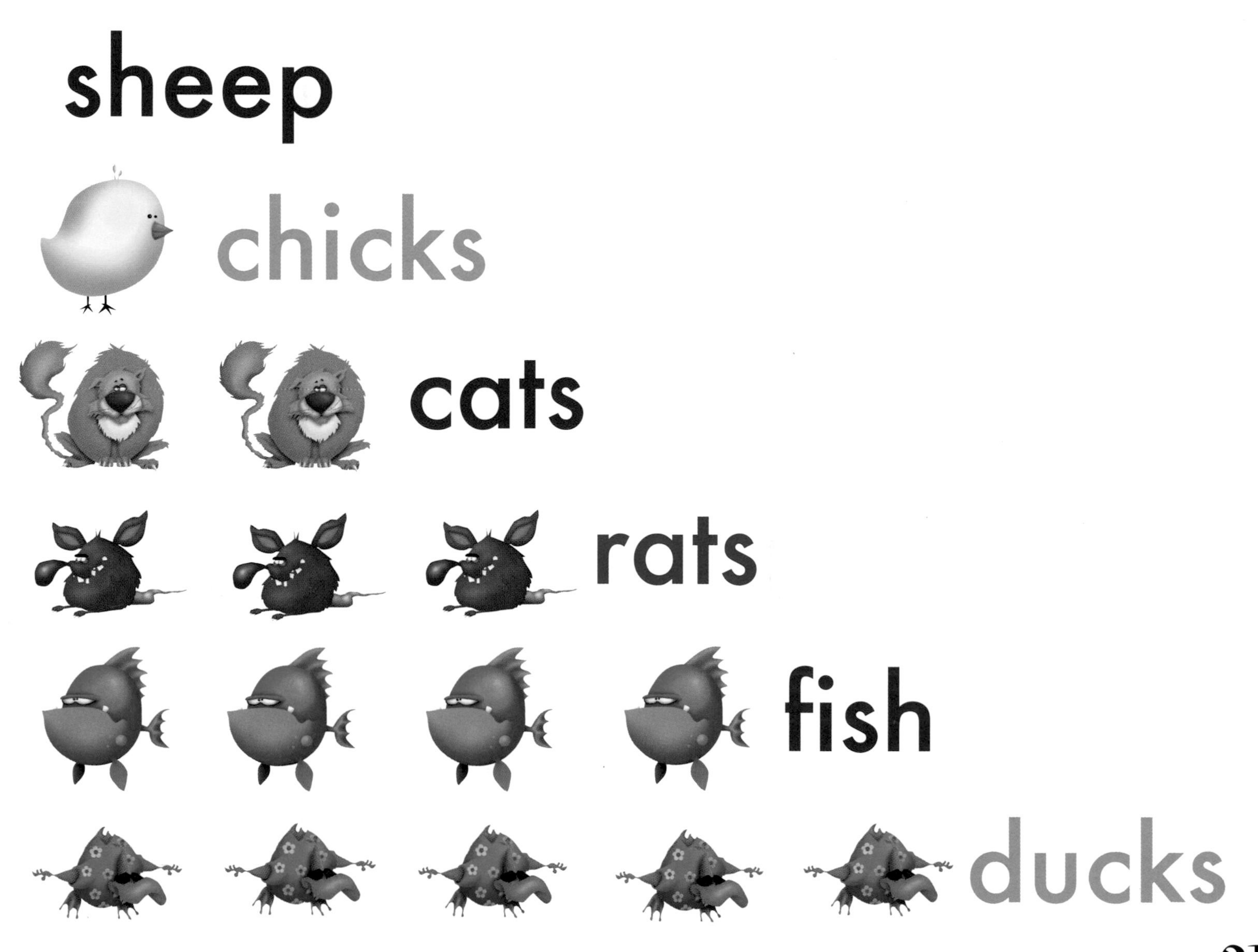

ABOUT THE AUTHORS AND ARTISTS

Ben Adams says farm animals are smelly, but he likes to draw pictures of them anyway. Ben lives in his very own house in Portland, Oregon. He likes to spend time in his backyard pruning, watering, and sculpting his trees into giant farm animals. Someday, he hopes to have his own tree farm and change his name to Farmer Ben.

Julie Hansen grew up in Tillamook, Oregon, and knows a lot about cows. Although she has never actually owned a cow, she has raised almost everything else: dogs, cats, chickens, rabbits, frogs, rats, mice, fish, ducks, snakes, squirrels, and the occasional muskrat. She lives in Salem, Oregon with her husband, Mark, their son, Chance, two cats, and a dog the size of a cat.

Kyle Holveck lives in Newberg, Oregon, with his wife, Raydene, and their daughter, Kylie. In Newberg, there are lots of farms and animals. Kyle's favorite farm animal is the rhinoceros, which *we* know is not really a farm animal. Because his house is too small to keep a rhinoceros, Kyle has a chihuahua named Pedro instead.

Aaron Peeples's hero is Farmer Bob. He says that any man who can look good wearing overalls day after day is definitely a great man. Aaron is currently attending college in Portland, Oregon, and he enjoys drawing farm animals at Flying Rhinoceros between classes.

Ray Nelson thinks cows and pigs are really neat. He also thinks bacon and hamburgers are really neat. (We haven't told him where bacon and hamburgers come from yet.) Ray lives in Wilsonville, Oregon, with his wife, Theresa. They have two children, Alexandria and Zach, and a mutant dog named Molly.

CONTRIBUTORS: Melody Burchyski, Jennii Childs, Paul Diener, Lynnea "Mad Dog" Eagle, MaryBeth Habecker, Mark Hansen, Lee Lagle, Mari McBurney, Mike McLane, Chris Nelson, Hillery Nye, Kari Rasmussen, Steve Sund, and Ranjy Thomas